Danielle Cole is a 56-year-old mother and grandmother. She has worked in the secondary education sector for over twenty years and has taken up writing as a hobby over the years for enjoyment. She started off writing short stories and illustrating them for her grandchildren to read at bedtime. Then she progressed into writing further fiction and decided, as her family found them intriguing to read, that she would send a novel she had written to a publisher.

Anthony

I would like to dedicate this book to my children, Christopher, William, Rhianne and Leigh for supporting me throughout and giving me the motivation to send it to a publisher. And also to my partner, Gary, and his boss, Chris O'Hara, for providing the financial support needed to get this book on the shelves.

with love
mom
2.
xoxox

Danielle Cole

SIXTEEN

AUSTIN MACAULEY PUBLISHERS™

LONDON • CAMBRIDGE • NEW YORK • SHARJAH

A CIP catalogue record for this title is available from the British Library.

ISBN 9781398422223 (Paperback)
ISBN 9781398422230 (ePub e-book)

www.austinmacauley.com

First Published (2021)
Austin Macauley Publishers Ltd
25 Canada Square
Canary Wharf
London
E14 5LQ

I would like to thank Austin Macauley Publishers for taking their time to read my novel and having the faith in it to see it through to be published.

The blue April sky was gradually turning a murky grey colour. The clouds were getting darker and darting furiously across the sky as if they were running away from something. Rain started to drip slowly; then without warning, the heavens opened. Big globules of rain splashed down to earth at a fast pace, soaking everything in its sight. Puddles started to form almost instantly as the rain was too heavy that the ground could not cope. The wind started to howl and pick up speed. An almighty crash was heard across the town. People scurried inside to get out of the rain. Cars drove slowly along the road with their wipers on full speed. A minute or so later, the sky lit up as a bolt of lightning hit. You could hear the buzz of the electricity going through it, even over the rain. This was going to be one of the worst storms ever recorded. Even though it was only just after four in the afternoon, you would think it was nearly ten instead as it was that dark and miserable.

The rain was relentless, coming down in sheets. The thunder and lightning continued for ages; a clap of thunder followed moments later by the lightening. For a photographer, the pictures would have been amazing; the sky was being lit up, as if you had set off a hundred fireworks all at once, but for the people of the town, it was terrifying. It seemed to be directly above them and for some people, it had already caused structural damage to their houses. The streets were almost empty that evening, except the odd worker returning home. No one wanted to go out and get soaked. Even the hardened dog walkers remained indoors.

Luckily for the residents of the town, the river ran on the outskirts and no buildings were nearby so when the river burst its banks and spilled out, no building would be in danger of flooding. The storm continued to rage through most of the night.

In the morning, the rain had finally stopped, and the blue skies had once more returned. People went out to inspect the damage that the storm had done. Fences had been blown down. Trees had been uprooted and lay across the road blocking it off. Roofs had lost tiles, which lay broken on the ground. The lightening had hit some of the houses, leaving gaping holes in the roof. The town soon came to life, with people cleaning up and repairing the damage. By the end of the day, the only things visible to say that there had even been a storm were the holes left by the uprooted trees and the very swollen river, which now appeared to be twice as wide as it was before. Sometime during the night, it had burst its banks. No one ventured down there, as the ground was sodden. It was more of a bog than a field now. Plus, the current was still running fast, so it was dangerous as well. It was a popular place for the dog walkers to go to as it was safe to let the dogs of the lead and let them have a good run.

The area was left undisturbed for a fortnight.

Ted got his dogs ready on their leads. It was about time they had a good run. Even if it was a bit muddy there, he could always bath them afterwards. The dogs were going as stir crazy as himself. He had missed his daily chats with the other dog walkers, especially Arthur. He lived on his own, his wife had died a few years ago and his children had moved out of the town, and although he saw them regularly, he was on his own most of the time. That was why he had bought a couple of dogs; to keep him company. Ted loved his dogs, Millie the cocker spaniel, and Scruff, the mongrel. He had got them from the dog centre for rescued and abandoned dogs. They had been found together and came as a pair. They were inseparable. They played together, ate together and slept together. Millie and Scruff almost pulled Ted to the field. They knew the way; they had been going there most days with Ted since they moved in with him. Once at the field, Ted unclipped their leads and let them have a much-needed run-about. The other dog walkers must have had the same thoughts as Ted as it wasn't long before he saw others. He chatted merrily to each one. People were still commentating on the storm. Ted was 73 years old and he said he had never heard or seen a storm so loud in his life. The ground was still soft and muddy in places and in some parts the grass was still flat. The force of the water when the banks burst had bulldozed over the grass and flattening it in its path. It wasn't long before Ted spotted Arthur. They walked along slowly talking whilst Millie, Scruff and Scamp, Arthur's dog, raced ahead. They all got on well and saw each other most days.

All of a sudden, Scamp came to a halt, his tail stopped wagging and he began to bark. Millie and Scruff went to investigate and they both joined in. The dogs had obviously found something. Ted and Arthur scurried over to the dogs to see what it was they were barking at. When the approached the dogs, they managed to shoo them away; if it was a dead animal of some kind, they didn't want the dogs to get ill from it. They were surprised and shocked to see a leg, complete with a boot on it, sticking out of the mud. At first, they thought it was a mannequin, but on closer inspection, they realised it was a human leg. Luckily, Arthur had a mobile phone on him and rang the police. They were instructed to stay nearby so the police could locate them and keep the dogs on their leads. The dogs were not happy about this and pulled and jerked on their leads until they realised it was fruitless and lay down by their masters' feet.

Inspector Robert Brown was first on the scene. He noted down Ted and Arthur's addresses and kindly asked them to leave, saying that someone would be around later to get a statement from each of them. Brown radioed through to the station to confirm it was a human leg and that he would need forensics and a backup team. DCI Thomas arrived next. He was not in the best of moods. This was his last few weeks at work; he was about to retire after 40 years on the force. Now he had this to deal with. He hoped and prayed that whatever this turned out to be, it wouldn't take long. If the leg was still attached to a body, then it could be down to the storm, the person could have drowned when the river burst. If that was the case, the paperwork would be at a minimal and he could still retire on his due date.

Forensics arrived ten minutes later. They set up a tent over the leg so no one could see what was going on. They set to work, carefully removing the earth around the leg that was still sticking out of the ground at a 45-degree angle. They worked methodically so as not to disturb anything that they would later rely on and need, if it were not an open and shut case.

Eventually, they had unearthed the rest of the body. It was a male and it was plainly clear that he had been shot. The bullet had gone straight through his forehead, leaving a gaping hole behind. He had been shot at close range. They transferred the body into a body bag and then onto a gurney. It was wheeled into the back of the waiting van, ready to be taken to the city morgue. The forensic guys took samples of earth from where the body was to see if they could get any clues from it.

By now, other police officers had turned up. They were carefully combing the area. DCI Thomas was barking out orders. He was angry. This was all he needed. He could almost feel his near grey hair getting greyer by the minute. He had always kept himself fit and prided himself in his appearance, but now as he stood in the field, his shoes covered in mud, he roughly put his hand through his hair and sighed. Why did this have to happen now, of all times?

PC Andrews shouted out that she had found something. Thomas snapped back into focus and stomped over to her and raged.

'This had better be good, Andrews. I want this case wrapped up quickly, do you hear me, quickly.'

Andrews glared at him but kept her mouth shut. His bark was worse than his bite. This was her first murder case, and she was already starting to feel queasy. She pointed to the finger that was just visible in the ground. Thomas bent down and carefully removed some of the mud with his gloved hand. It revealed more fingers. He called to the two forensic guys to come over at once.

Thomas looked at Andrews and felt for her. She was young, not long out of training. She had gone pale and he knew if she stood and watched the body being unearthed, she would be physically sick, but then again, she needed to watch, get the first dead body over and done with. In this line of work, this would not be her last body that she would see. He remembered his first body that he had seen. It was a young male who had been driving at speed and had lost control of his car, which had flipped over several times, before coming to rest in a ditch. The air bag had gone off with such a force that it had suffocated the young man. He would have died anyway, if not for the airbag, as there were many bones that had broken, including ribs, which had, in turn, punctured his lungs. The car must have rolled over a good few many times. It hadn't been a pretty sight, legs and arms bent at peculiar angles and bones protruding out of the skin. He had done all the necessary checks before vomiting. Over the years, he got to accept that it was all part of the job, but he never got used to it. Each one had made him feel sick. He could see that Andrews wanted to move away but he made her stay. She needed to get this out of the way if she was going to make it in the force.

Once again, the forensics worked slowly and methodically. Andrews watched them work. As they started to lift the body out of its shallow grave, she looked away. She could feel the bile rising to her throat. It burnt and she gagged.

The forensic guys beckoned to Thomas to come and have a look before they put the body on a trolley and send it to the morgue. Once again, it was a male who had been shot straight through the forehead.

Thomas let out a loud sigh. Now he had two dead bodies on his hands. The nausea finally took hold of Andrews and she violently threw up. Thomas patted her on her back and said:

'You'll be fine now, that's the first dead body out of the way, it doesn't get any easier, but you somehow get used to it and cope.'

Andrews wiped her mouth on a tissue she had retrieved from her pocket, smiled and walked away. She thought to herself, *I'll never get used to it!*

She hadn't walked far when she tripped over something and fell face forward into the mud. Thomas ran over to her to over her assistance and also to reprimand her for being careless and not looking where she was going. He saw that she was lying next to yet another body. She had tripped over an arm that was laying in her path. He quickly yanked her up and called to the forensics that they had better get over here. He tore Andrews off a strip, reminding her that this was a crime scene and she needed to be more alert, before storming off.

By now, a few other forensics had turned up and so had half the force. They were combing the area, walking at a snail's pace, eyes firmly fixed on the ground, moving the debris from the flood carefully out the way using a long stick to do so and checking it out.

The arm sticking out of the mud belonged to a man that had also been shot the through the forehead. Now there were three dead bodies.

Thomas was now beside himself. He was fuming.

By the time evening came and it started getting darker, they had uncovered 11 bodies in total. All of them males and all with a bullet through their foreheads. This was an execution of some sort.

Thomas was incensed. He hadn't got much longer left; he had been looking forward to his retirement. Now he would

15

have to put that on hold until things were sorted with this case. He wouldn't and couldn't leave it unsolved or for someone else to solve it. He had been married to the police force all his adult life and was not going to abandon it now.

The bodies were all transported to the morgue to await autopsies. Thomas had ordered the pathologist to give them priority over anything else. As there were so many bodies, the pathologist managed to draft in others from other towns to assist. One by one, the bodies were examined. The mud, which had concealed the bodies, was like a form of peat and that had helped to preserve the bodies.

There were ligature marks around all of their wrists and ankles, evidence that they had all been tightly bound. There were also marks in each corner of their mouths, which indicated that they had been gagged. All eleven of them had been males at varying ages and had been shot at close range. It appeared that the bindings had been removed after death due to the colouration of the skin. Fibres, prints and dental moulds were taken. Not one of them had any identification on them.

The place had been cordoned off with the official yellow police tape, which was now blowing in the wind. It had been a long day for all of them. They were all told to go home and get some rest as everyone was feeling exhausted.

Andrews couldn't wait to get home and a have a long soak in a hot bath. She had felt tainted ever since falling over the arm. She had even started to doubt her choice of career. Her father and grandfather had been police officers. She had so desperately wanted to follow in their footsteps; she had wanted to make them as proud of her as she was of them.

Andrews walked through the door of her apartment and flicked the button on her answer machine, as it was flashing red, so she could listen to the messages whilst she ran her bath. There were three messages. The first one was from the telephone engineer enquiring into how she was finding everything, the second was from a call centre about energy bills, saying they would ring back another time but the third one made the hairs on the back of neck stand to attention.

'You have heard of me, but you don't know me, well, not properly. I have been watching you and thought that I might, might I say again, give your career a needed boost. You and the rest of the team have managed to unearth 11 of my bodies but let me tell you my favourite number is 16. Let's see if that little bit of information will earn you a brownie point or two, or not.'

The line had then gone dead. She checked the call back list and found that the last number had been withheld. She rang the station, hoping that Thomas was still there. He was. She told him about the message. She could feel her voice cracking as she relayed what it had said. He told her to make sure her doors and windows were secure and that he would be over straight away. He told her not to answer the door to anyone until he was there.

Twenty minutes later, Thomas and Andrews stood side by side in her front room, listening to the message. They replayed it a dozen times to see if they could hear any background noises. Nothing.

Thomas could see how on edge Andrews was; she had tried holding her feelings back but eventually the tears fell. Thomas held her like a father would a child, after all, her own father was dead, he had died in action, he had been his partner,

17

he almost felt he owed her. Once her tears had been spent, he told her to get her bath and freshen up whilst he ordered them both some food. He was going to stay with her for the time being. He lived alone so he had no reason to rush back to his place.

Andrews returned a little while later relaxed and dressed in a lounge suit. Her hair was loosely pinned up. Thomas looked up at her and smiled. She was so alike her father, those big blue eyes with their long eyelashes, it was like looking at her father's eyes all over again. She had the same lithe build as him as well and even in a lounge suit, she looked attractive. He loved this woman, not in a sexual way but as a father figure. He had known her most of her life, he had seen her grow up as her father had been his partner. The two of them had not only been partners they were friends, good friends.

The food arrived. They dished it up and sat down to eat. Andrews opened up a bottle of wine; it wasn't often she had a drink, but after the day, they had she felt they could do with it. Together, they ate, drank and spoke about the day and the message. Whilst Andrews cleared away when they had finished eating, Thomas made some calls. He called one of the police technicians and asked for him to come to Andrews to put a tracer on her phone in case she received any more calls. He also wanted her phone connected to his in his office so they could keep a constant check on things just in case this person rang back.

They spoke some more, mainly about her father before he left. He had wanted to stay on the settee for the night as he felt the need to protect her and make sure she was safe. He had felt a sense of duty to shield her as soon as she had enrolled to train as a police officer, but she had insisted that she was okay now and that she was a big girl now. He had made her promise that she would bolt the door and windows when he left. Although he didn't like it, he felt a little more reassured when the technician had been and put the tracer on her phone.

Thomas rose early the next morning. He showered and ate his normal cereal that he had every morning before work and left his house. As he drove along the road, he had a strange instinct wash over him to tell him to drive past Andrew's apartment. As he approached, he could see her car still in its parking lot. He rang her number and she answered it on the third ring. Thomas breathed a sigh of relief. He didn't wait for an invite for coffee, he just told her to put the coffee pot on.

When he reached her door, he saw etched into the wood: the number 16. He could see that it had been freshly done. Well, he hadn't left until almost midnight and it was only half six in the morning. Someone was obviously watching her apartment. Thomas told her to pack a bag as he felt she wasn't safe staying there on her own at the moment. At first, she tried to put up a fight, but this was one she wasn't going to win. She knew how stubborn Thomas could be, after all, she had known him for years; her dad had often bought him back to their home for meals, parties etc., he was almost like family, every celebration the Andrews household had, Thomas was always part of it. She went and packed some items to last three or four days, just in case.

They arrived at the station in different cars. Thomas wanted a tracker to be placed on her car and had organised it on his way to work. As Andrews drove through the gate, she was asked to relinquish her keys so they could fit it at once. They didn't want Thomas getting on at them for not being prompt, they had felt his wrath before and it wasn't nice.

They had a briefing, which Thomas chaired. He told them about the voice message on Andrew's home phone and the number 16 etched into her door. He showed them a detailed map of the area where the 11 bodies had been found. He had divided the rest of the area around them into equal sizes and allocated two officers to each of them. So far, the press had kept away but it was only a matter of time before they were sniffing around for information. They were all told not to say anything to anyone, especially the press.

Thomas left with Andrews to get the statements from Ted and Arthur. They left the other officers to start the search. The statements didn't take long, as there was not a lot to tell them, just two men taking their dogs for a walk and the dogs barking at a leg sticking out of the ground. They had rung the police straight away, they hadn't touched anything and they were sure that their dogs had either, and once the police hadn't turned up, they had left. They handwrote the statements, read it back to each of them and then got them to sign in the appropriate places. They left and went to the morgue to see how the autopsies were going.

It had taken most of the day to search the area. Every millimetre of each square had been gone over with a fine-tooth comb and nothing had been found. They were starting to feel hungry and thirsty, and the sun had gone behind the clouds, leaving the air cold. They were about to give up and go back to the station when PC Fletcher, Fletch for short, said he was desperate for the toilet and as the tree was nearer, he was going behind that and for them to wait for him. On his way back, he saw the 12th body. As the river water had gone down giving the land back up, it had left the body exposed to the elements. It was in a bad state, as insects had already started to feast on it. Fletch whistled to get their attention and soon forensics were once again returning to the site to collect yet another body.

Thomas knew they had found another body before it had been radioed in as the interceptor put on Andrew's phone, went through to the one set up in his office, leaving another message.

'Congratulations on finding Number 12, four more to go.'

It was too short to trace where it had come from. Thomas knew that whoever was responsible was lurking around the area watching and waiting. How else would they know that another body had been found? He scratched his head; all the officers had been told to make sure they didn't talk to anyone and that no one was allowed to come anywhere near the area. It was all to be cordoned off to avoid people having a nose. He trusted his team so he quickly shrugged off the thought that one of colleagues could be a mole.

Thomas drove him and Andrews down to the site. He spoke to his team about the message. This time they searched nearer to the river edge. Hidden in the bulrushes was Body 13. This one was different to the rest. It was a child. Same marks around the wrists, ankles and mouth, same bullet hole in the forehead, but it had been weighted down the bulrushes so that it couldn't move. Again, the body was badly decomposed. Andrews thought that she would be sick but the anger she felt against whoever had done this, especially to a child, managed to stop her.

Thomas and Andrews walked in silence along the riverbank and to their sheer horror, found bodies 14 and 15. Another child and a woman, both weighed down.

Two weeks later the bodies had been identified, mainly through the use of their dental records and Interpol. Five of them had been from Latvia. One of the identified was a politician of high standing. The press had now got wind of something serious going on and were all over it like bees to a honey pot. It wasn't long before they were printing stories about numerous bodies being discovered in their daily newspapers. Luckily, the press still knew nothing about the 16th body that was supposedly still to be found. No one on his team had leaked the information that was told them about the voice message. Everywhere you went, people were talking about it; it was the topic of the town, it was in the papers and on the news.

Thomas's phone rang; this time he picked it up on the first ring and beckoned Andrews to speak.

'Hello, who is this?' she said as calmly as possible.

'Shut up and listen, I ask the questions, not you, Body 16 hasn't been found yet and that is because it is still walking around. Find out why these people had to go, then you won't have to find Body 16, you have five days to do it,' came a distorted voice.

With that, the line went dead. The call was traced to a burner phone just outside the police station. By the time an officer got to the location, no one was around except a chalked message on the pavement: 5 days, and the remnants of a mobile phone, which was in pieces over the path.

The team worked hard on finding out everything they could, especially on the Latvian politician, his family, friends, associates, his party and his connections with Britain. His wife and two children were among those dead and also his brother.

Everything they found out about him was nothing that would warrant him and his family to be executed. He had been a model student at school, he had come from a respectable family. He had married his childhood sweetheart and had remained faithful to her, likewise her to him. He had gone into politics by mistake standing up for the people of Latvia and everyone spoke highly of him. No one had a bad word to say about him. Every stone that Thomas and his team upturned led them to a blank. They hadn't got to dwell on things, one day had already gone past making various calls to various people, finding out what they could about the deceased.

Thomas called an emergency meeting before dismissing them.

'Right, everyone, this is what we know so far. Boris was a politician; he was well liked by other politicians as well as the locals. Martyna was his wife, and they had two children, Tomsk, aged 12, and Marianna, aged 10. His brother Stephan worked for Boris as an advisor. The others were all British and were at various stages in their lives and careers. None of them were politicians. Charlie was a pub landlord with no criminal record, Bob was a retired banker, again no criminal record, the twins, Dave and Trevor, were small-time criminals and didn't work. Eddie had done time in prison for armed robbery and drug offences but since his release, he had been on the straight and narrow, so to speak, he was still on the police radar but there was nothing to stick to him, although it was still believed that he was dealing drugs again. Joe, John and Jordan, three brothers, had run their own butcher's shop and had not been in any trouble all their lives, they were well known and had a bit of reputation to being racist and cruel towards others. Frank and Warren were both unemployed and had no fixed abode.'

There was nothing to tie one to the other.

'I've put their pictures on the board and written underneath what we know about each one so far. If anyone has anything else to add, then let me know so we can add it on the board.' He paused for a while, then added, 'Think about what we know so far and what could their connection be with each other. We will resume again at 7:30 am sharp.'

A few of them went to the local pub afterwards but Thomas stayed in the office. The press had been virtually camped outside the front door of the station and he couldn't be bothered with them. The phone in his office went off. He let it go to the answer machine.

'Time is running out; you have four days left. I don't think you will find out why these people had to die, so you will retire knowing that you could have saved Number 16 and you will leave without solving a major crime.'

Thomas scratched his head. No one except a handful in the force knew that he was going to retire. He went over all the findings from the forensic teams. No bullet casings had been found and no bullets had been found lodged in the bodies of the deceased. Whoever had shot them shot them at close range and the bullet had gone straight through and out the other side. There were no fingerprints on any of the bodies. The only thing that had been found were fibres from the rope that the bound the victim's legs and arms and a couple of tiny fibres from whatever had been used to gag them. They had run the rope fibres through the database to match it up and to find out its origin. He looked at the name of the rope again, zylon rope 25mm thick. He had heard of this before, but from where? He sat for a good half an hour, racking his brains trying to figure out where he had seen this rope previously. He couldn't think. His mind was foggy. He had too many thoughts running through his head all at once; who was the killer or killers? The rope, who knew he was going to retire? And how did they get Andrews' private phone number? She was ex-directory.

Andrews walked in and startled him. He had been deep in thought and hadn't heard her walk up to him. He jumped. Andrews laughed nervously, and said:

'I have bought you some sandwiches and a coffee, as I knew you would still be working when you didn't turn up at the pub.'

Thomas aired his views with Andrews, telling her that he thought it could be a member of the team that could have done this. They would know he was retiring; they could have got her phone number from the database if it had been put on or she could have given it out to people, and they would have known to get rid of any bullet casings. At first, she thought Thomas was losing his mind but the more she thought about it, the more the idea seemed to fit. The phone calls were either too short to trace, or when they had been traced, it was to a burner phone that was destroyed afterwards. Together, they looked at each member of the team, bringing their full name, address, date of birth, next of kin, all the normal HR rubbish that you have to provide. Then there was a box for promotions, special awards, bravery and such.

At first, nothing unusual stood out; each member of the team had something in the latter box, some more than others. They went through which member was where on the field and by the river, who had found what and how they had found them. They made notes and compared them with each other. Andrews turned to Thomas, and said:

'The only name that sticks out to me is Fletch. He left his post to go for a wee behind a tree, he didn't use the portaloos that were erected in the field, saying the tree was nearer and he was desperate. It might have been nearer; I don't know, though.'

'Well, in his statement, he said he went to the tree as he couldn't wait any longer,' Thomas replied.

'If you look at his profile, there is no next of kin and he has been overlooked for promotion more than once,' Andrews stated.

'I see what you are saying, Andrews, but why a Latvian politician and his family? I just don't get it. Say it is Fletch, what would be the connection with him?' Thomas said quietly.

They were both tired and decided to call it a night; it was getting late. They would look at it again in the morning. They would both be watching Fletch without telling anyone else of their concerns. When Thomas walked up to his front door, he noticed a 16 painted on it, big and bold.

This had to be someone who knew both him and Andrews, they knew where they both lived. This was now getting personal. They had not only invaded Andrew's privacy; they or someone had done so to his now. He was furious.

He poured himself a large brandy and sat in his armchair, listening for any noise whilst all manner of thoughts danced through his head.

Thomas eventually drifted off into a fitful sleep, still sitting in his armchair. He had had another couple of brandies before finally the tiredness took hold.

He woke with a start. He could smell burning. He shot up out of his armchair and noticed that a fire was taking hold in his kitchen, it had already engulfed the back door. Thomas fumbled around for his phone and door keys whilst choking on the smoke that was now getting thick and filling up his front room. He ran out onto the street and rang the fire brigade. The firemen were able to put the fire out pretty quickly. The kitchen was completely gutted, and the living room wasn't too bad, it had only just started to take hold in there, so it was more smoke and water damage than anything else. The fire inspector was there and told Thomas that it was deliberate arson. Torched into the lawn in the back garden was a number 16.

Once the place was given the all-clear and Thomas was given permission to re-enter his property, he went in and packed a bag. He knew until this was over, he would not be staying there again. He thought about Andrews. What if it had been her apartment, how would she have got out; there was only one entrance. He tried to dismiss these thoughts but try as he could they kept flashing before him. He could see her at the window, bashing it with all her might and screaming for help. Every time he seemed to blink, he could see this vision. He decided to drive there; it was three in the morning, so the roads were quiet. It wouldn't take him long to get there if he put his foot down. When he pulled up in her street, he could see the blue flashing lights of a fire engine and police cars. He knew straight away that her apartment had been targeted as well. He parked up and sprinted towards her block. The fireman stood in the way and then a policeman came over and said:

'Sorry, sir, it's too dangerous, you need to stand back in case the windows of the adjoining apartments blow.'

Thomas told the police officer that he was a DCI and showed him his badge. He told him that one of his team, PC Andrews lived in that apartment. The officer told him that the residents had all been evacuated and that the fire brigade had checked the building and had found no one else in there.

Thomas gave a sigh of relief. He looked around and noticed that her car wasn't in the parking lot. He gave the fire inspector his direct mobile number after telling them who he was and asked him to call him as soon as he knew the exact cause of the fire.

Thomas was too wide awake now. He found a café that was open 24 hours and ordered a black coffee. He needed to clear his head If this was a deliberate attempt on his and Andrews' life, then there had to be a reason or a connection.

He hugged the mug of steaming coffee in both hands and slowly sipped the black liquid. He could feel the warmth trickle down his throat. His thoughts were going faster than a dozen cars at Brans Hatch. He could not switch off. He ordered a fresh coffee and poached egg on toast with some bacon. He realised he was famished. All he had eaten yesterday was his cereal in the morning and the sandwich that Andrews had bought him. Once he had finished, he left the waitress a generous tip and drove to work.

The security guard on the gate was surprised to see him so early and said:

'Morning, sir, I didn't expect to see you this early after you left so late last night, are you okay?'

Thomas didn't want to have idle chit chat with him, so he just smiled and said he was fine and had a lot to do.

Thomas fired up his computer and opened his emails. Most of them were unimportant but one of them stood out like a sore thumb. It was from an unknown source and marked urgent and important. The subject was *four days*.

Thomas opened it up immediately. There were two pictures of burning buildings, on closer inspection he realised that one was his house and the other was Andrew's apartment. Underneath the picture of his house was a caption, *Nearly 16* and underneath Andrew's apartment was, *Would have been 16 if she had been home*.

Thomas glared at the screen and slammed his hand hard onto his desk. What was he missing?

Andrews walked in just before 7:30; she looked like hell. She had been woken up in the early hours of the morning to say her apartment was on fire. By the time she had driven around there, the fire was well alight, and she knew that all her possessions would have been burnt, destroyed. She was just about to tell Thomas all about it when the chief of fire rang Thomas's phone. He confirmed that it was arson. It had been started deliberately by someone pouring an inflammable liquid through the letter box and setting light to it. Thomas thanked God that Andrews had not been at home as she would have been burnt to death; there would have been no escape route, and according to the fireman, the place was soon engulfed in flames. She wouldn't have stood a chance. Thomas shuddered at the thought of her being trapped like he had seen in his visions. He thanked the officer and hung up.

He looked at Andrews and went to break the news to her about her apartment, presuming that she didn't know about the fire. When she told him that she had received a call saying it was on fire and that she had raced around there he turned to her.

'So where have you been staying, then? Who phoned you?' he was starting to suspect everyone now; she could be holding a grudge on him that why did he survive, and her father was killed.

Andrews told him that she had stayed away since the message on her answer machine and then the 16 being etched in her door the following morning. She told him she had taken his advice and had booked into a hotel; she hadn't told anyone which hotel, as she was scared that it was someone who knew her.

Thomas turned around, and said nastily, 'You're lying to me, you were seen driving into your parking lot.'

'I did pop back, I had forgotten something, I was literally in and out, two minutes was all it took to get what I needed. So, I apologise for not giving you an updated account of my every move,' she snarled back.

'Look, I'm sorry for even the slightest accusation towards you and the manner in which I spoke to you, I didn't mean anything by it, it's just that one, I worry about you and two, we have only four days left, I don't know who Body 16 will be. I've been doing this job for 40 years and not one case had got by me, I've solved each and everyone. I just thought that you might have told me where you were staying,' he said humbly.

'I'm sorry too, the message spooked me as you know, and I didn't want to sound childish that's why I insisted that you went that night. I jumped at every noise that night and hardly slept. Then when you turned up the following morning and told me about the door, I couldn't believe that I hadn't heard anything. I went back, as I told you, to get something important and left. The next thing I know, someone rang me of a withheld number to tell me my apartment was on fire. As I was pulling out of my street, I thought I saw your car pulling in so I was beginning to think it was something to do with you,' she said quietly.

'Can I ask you one more question?' Thomas asked.

'Sure.'

'What was so important that you risked going back there?'

'A framed picture of my dad, I never go anywhere without that picture and in my haste to get out of there, I forgot to pack it.'

'I think we have both got our wires crossed this morning, I think it's the stress of this mess. Ever since you signed up as a trainee in the force, I have kept an eye on you. I asked for all your reports to be sent to me on how you were doing. I was so proud when I was told you had excelled in all aspects of the training, especially the fitness one. Your dad would have been proud too, he was an excellent runner and athlete, you sure do take after him. I stuck my neck on the line to make sure I got you on my team,' Thomas said rather shyly, especially for a man of his standing.

'Why?' Andrews asked, alarmed at this confession.

'Because I owe it to your father, he was partner, my best friend, he was killed in the line of duty as you know. That bullet he took should have been mine. He had a wife and a family, I had no one. I felt responsible and now I feel that for you, responsible.'

Andrews now fell into his arms and sobbed. Through her tears, she managed to say that she was so glad that she had gone back to the apartment and got the photo as now everything was destroyed in the fire. He held her for a while, he felt sorry for her, he had uninvertible accused her and she knew he had and then she had risked her life by getting that photo. He handed her some tissues and walked away.

After pulling himself together, he addressed the others.

Briefing was kept to a minimal that morning, the emphasis was finding the location of who sold the rope, who purchased it. It should stick in the mind of the seller, as it would have been a large quantity for tying up 15 people.

He took Andrews to one side after everyone had left and told her about his house being torched and the number sixteens found at both fires.

Someone somewhere had linked the two of them together and had tried to destroy one or the other. But what was the link between one of them and the other victims? He didn't know any of them and neither did Andrews.

Day two was largely taken up with looking for the supplier of the rope. They had narrowed it down to two supplies and officers were dispatched to both locations to interview the owners and go through their sales books and hopefully CCTV cameras.

At 4 pm Thomas' radio went off to let him know that they had found who had supplied the rope. A man had rung up the shop on an unknown number and ordered it stating how much he wanted, and the thickness of the rope and he would be in later and he had the cash to buy it. When the owner had asked for a name, he had been told its Mr Smith, no initials, just Mr Smith. Thomas asked if they had any camera footage of this Mr Smith entering the shop and was disappointed when told that the shop didn't have any fitted. The shop on one side was vacant and the other was closed, whilst the owner was on holiday and wouldn't be back for another six days.

Thomas put down his radio and sighed loudly. Day two was coming to an end and they were no nearer. The rope had drawn a blank. All they had was where it had been bought from, no name, no CCTV footage. Boy, this man or men who have done this terrible thing are or were clever he thought. This shop had obviously been chosen for the rope, as it was out of the way and didn't have cameras to pick anyone up when someone would leave after a purchase. The only thing that came out of it was if the person was working alone then they must be fit to be able such a large quantity of heavy rope. Thomas had been pinning his hopes on this rope. He looked across at Andrews, who was now fully composed since her meltdown this morning. He shook his head in despair when she asked if they had any success.

They left the station together that evening and decided to go and get some food together. They went to the little restaurant not far from the station. It was quiet in there this time of day. They wouldn't be disturbed and could eat and talk in peace. They both needed something to eat, even though neither were feeling like eating. Andrews hadn't eaten all day and Thomas hadn't had anything since his poached egg on toast and bacon.

The place only had a handful of other diners. They found a table tucked away in the corner and looked at the menu. A waiter came over to take their order not long afterwards. Andrews ordered a warm chicken salad with freshly baked bread and Thomas ordered his normal steak, medium rare and ordered some wine for them both. They spoke in hushed tones about the day and what they were going to do next until their food arrived. They ate and drank in silence. Each deep in thought about what was going on, what had already happened and what could possibly happen next.

The waiter broke their silence as he approached them. He coughed and apologised for having to disturb them and handed them a brown manila envelope. He said that a young lad had handed it to him, asking for him to give it to a Thomas or an Andrews. Thomas thanked him and took the envelop from him.

The pair of them looked at the envelop for a while before Thomas opened it. Inside was a letter made up of words cut out from newspapers and magazines. It read:

Day two over, three to go then boom
I am too clever for you both no paper trail
Nothing
Soon you will have body 16

Thomas got out his mobile and phoned through to the station.

A member of the forensic team, Matt, turned up moments later and collected the envelope from Thomas, and told him he would work on it straight way. Matt took the envelop back to the lab and started his investigation. He checked the whole envelope and the letter for fingerprints. The only ones visible were Thomas's and what turned out to be the waiters. Matt found his prints on their database as he had been caught drunk driving about five years previously. He checked the gum on the envelope for saliva and that turned up nothing. Nothing was found on the cut-out letters and words and the glue used to stick them down was everyday PVA glue. Nothing about that envelop and letter held any clues.

Thomas and Andrews couldn't eat anymore. The contents of the envelop had unnerved them and any feeling of hunger had vanished.

Andrews went up to the waiter and asked to see the manager. The waiter, thinking he was in trouble for doing something wrong or there was something wrong with the food, tried to say the manager wasn't there today. Andrews showed him her police ID badge and he soon back tracked. The manager appeared within moments. Andrews asked to see the security camera tapes straight away. Thomas had already asked the desk sergeant at the station to check their cameras as the boy must have walked past there to get to the restaurant as the other side was a dead end.

They watched as the camera rolled, they saw themselves enter and then a black car left from the other side of the road. It drove at speed. The numberplate wasn't visible and as the car looked as if it had been modified, it was hard to tell what sort of make or model it was. 20 minutes or so later, they saw the young lad of about 12 or 13 walking into the restaurant. In his hand was the envelop. They watched the tape for a further half an hour and the only things they saw was the boy walking back out and a couple of diners coming into the restaurant. The car didn't return and no one else walked by.

The cameras at the police station had only picked up the same.

They thanked the manager and left. First, they went to Thomas' car to retrieve his bag, then they walked slowly to the hotel Andrews was staying in. Thomas had rung them earlier and had booked the adjacent room to hers for the foreseeable future. After all, he couldn't go back to his house yet. His kitchen was destroyed, and downstairs was either smoke or water damaged, and he hadn't had time to sort things out. That would have to wait until this was over. At least he had packed some clothes so he could get changed. He would have hated to wear the same clothes two days in a row. He had always kept himself immaculate and well kept.

They parted ways outside their rooms and went in to shower.

Andrews stood under the hot spray of water for ages, letting the water run down her body in little rivers. She hummed to herself as she washed. She felt relaxed. She knew Thomas was close by, and if he stuck by what he had said this morning of protecting her in honour of her father, then she would be safe. She got out and wrapped the big white fluffy towel around her body and the smaller one around her long hair. She felt better for the shower. She was looking forward to jumping into bed. She dried herself and towel dried her hair, she hadn't got the strength or energy to use the hairdryer; she was too tired.

In the room next door, Thomas had showered and shaved and was already asleep in his bed. He had virtually fallen asleep the moment his head hit the pillow. He hadn't been asleep for more than 20 minutes when he was woken by a blood curdling scream. He darted out of bed and raced to Andrew's door, where she stood draped in her towel, trembling and pale. She couldn't speak. Thomas pushed past her and saw that next to her bed was the number 16 drawn out with rose petals. This was serious. He scooped her up into his arms and carried her into his room and carefully laid her on the bed. He then rang down to reception, demanding that they get a doctor to come to his immediately. He was fuming. He had watched her go into her room and had heard the lock. Who had come into her room and how had they got in? All the time they waited for the doctor to arrive, she shook violently and sobbed quietly. He caressed her hair like a father would to his sick child and spoke in a whisper.

'I will get to the bottom of this and I will make them pay, I swear I will.'

The doctor came and gave her a sedative and she soon fell asleep. Thomas had already phoned the station and had got an officer to stand outside the hotel room on guard. He was under strict instructions not to let anyone in, not even the hotel staff unless Thomas was present first. He then went down to the reception. He was fuelled with rage. He demanded answers as to how someone could get into her room, which he knew for certain was locked.

'How can someone get into someone's room without a security pass is what I want to know!' he raged at the receptionist.

The receptionist told him that she had been on the desk all evening and hadn't given any passes out to that floor. With that Thomas demanded that the manager had better come to reception and check his CCTV cameras and a list of people who had recently stayed in that particular room and might have forgotten to hand in their pass on departure.

He got no concrete answers. The security camera for their floor was faulty so the images were very grainy. They could see a figure going in and coming out, but it was too badly distorted to zoom in to get a close up look of who it could be. This was getting more bizarre by the minute. Thomas went back to his room and checked on Andrews; she was sleeping peacefully after her sedative. He half slept in the chair, every so often waking and checking on her. She didn't stir all night.

It was now day three. Thomas had showered quickly and put on fresh clothes, brushed his teeth and hair and went to the station. He had made sure that the changeover of the officer keeping guard was done before leaving.

Forensics had managed to trace one of the fibres from the gags. They had been working flat out to find out where it had come from. Thomas received a call from the head of forensics and was totally knocked sideways when they told him that it had come from a regulation shirt from a uniform, a police shirt to be precise. Thomas kept that information to himself for now. He wanted to see if any of his team were getting itchy feet and by sharing this information, he could send them into panic mode, then he just might have body 16 on his hands before day five had even begun.

Thomas watched Fletch like a hawk all day. He had requested that he worked with him, especially in the absence of Andrews. Fletch was naturally nervous working head-to-head with his boss. He wanted to impress him and was on edge all day, making sure he didn't put a foot wrong or say a wrong thing.

Thomas was sure that Fletch was their man. No more calls or emails all day. Surely that couldn't just be a coincidence. Even when Fletch had visited the men's room he had followed him, so he had no direct access to send any messages, plus he had plenty of access to police shirts and probably owned quite a few.

Thomas went through lists of officers who had recently ordered shirts and those who might have a grudge against either Andrews or himself.

Nothing came up. Not a bean, a clue or even a tiny hint. Thomas was getting agitated. He was just about to swipe everything off his desk and thump Fletch in anger when his computer pinged. An email.

'You are barking up the wrong tree, you need to look closer to yourself.'

Each time he had received an email, it had been from a different email address which had been shut down as soon as it had been sent. Whoever was doing this was also a whizz kid with computers and technology. Fletch was off the hook. For one, he was with Thomas all day and he was sat right next to him when the email pinged through, and two, he had about as much nous with technology as did Thomas, who was like a fossil compared to the younger generation. A four-year-old would know more about computers than he did!

Thomas called an emergency briefing. He had just received news from Latvia.

Artis, the general secretary, had just got off the phone with him.

Thomas stood at the front and said:

'Right everyone, listen up. According to Artis, who is the general secretary for Latvia, Boris was one of the politicians for the Unity Party. Boris was popular and loved by everyone who met him. He had come to England with his wife, his two children and his brother. Apparently, his brother was going to meet someone in England and Boris had thought it a good idea to come with him and use the time sightseeing. He had wanted to come to England for a while now, so this was a good opportunity. Also, he could give his brother some moral support when he went to meet this person and find out what they wanted. The Latvian police are at present trying to find out what they can through his laptop at work and his private one, as well as a detailed search of his home. They are also doing the same thing with the brother's laptop and house. Artis has promised that this is being given the highest priority and that no stone will go unturned.'

Thomas added:

'If anyone knows anybody with Latvian connections, let me know, I will be in my office.' He then stomped off to his office, slamming the door behind him.

Andrews was still being guarded in her hotel room. She woke up feeling groggy from the sedative and it took her a while to work out where she was. When she actually realised where she was, the fears washed over like a tsunami. She shook from head to toe and snuggled down under the blankets. She tried to close her eyes but the number 16 kept dancing in front of her, tormenting her. Andrews got out of bed and tiptoed to the door. She gingerly opened it a fraction, just enough for her to peer outside. She saw a uniformed police office on guard. She felt a little more at ease at the sight of that and carefully shut the door again. She saw some clothes belonging to her on the dresser and decided to get dressed.

Meanwhile, Webster had gone in to see Thomas. Webster told him that the new guy, Dumesh had a Latvian connection. Thomas sprang from his chair and went to the area that was shared by the officers to look for him He wasn't there. He hadn't been in. In fact, he hadn't been in for the last few days. There was nothing anyone could do as HR had not uploaded his details yet due to the Easter holidays and they had probably forgotten to do it when they returned. He was incensed and said aloud that heads would roll if anything happened to Andrews or himself or any other officer for that matter by Dumesh through their incompetence of not putting his details on the database. There was nothing Thomas could do. He would have to wait until the morning and hope that Dumesh would turn in.

Thomas shut up his computer and went to the hotel. He found Andrews sitting on the bed. She smiled instantly as he walked through the door and she thanked him for setting up the guard. Thomas then went on to tell her about what Webster had said about Dumesh and that he wasn't in work. Andrews turned to Thomas and said:

'There is something strange about Dumesh, he has been with us for only a couple of weeks, he hasn't said from which force he has been transferred from, although he said it was a transfer to a couple of us. He hasn't formed any relationships with anyone, and he keeps looking at his phone all the time.'

Thomas said they were onto it, but they would have to wait. No details were on the database. It was almost as if he didn't exist. Thomas had even got the chief of police to check the national data base for his name. Nothing had come up. It looked likely that Dumesh was their man.

Day four started like every other morning, with the standard briefing for the day. Thomas told his team about Dumesh which got everyone talking. No one had seen him for days, no one had heard from him, which wasn't surprising really as he hadn't made friends with anyone enough to give out his number or get anyone else's. He hadn't even phoned into the main switchboard to report his absence either.

The technicians were already working on Dumesh's laptop. Every patrol officer was out looking for him. The police artist had drawn up a photo fit of him and it had been sent to everyone. Everyone was hell bend on finding him.

They all knew that time was running out. At 14:36, Thomas' email box pinged. He quickly opened it up. Again, it was from an unknown source and was headed Webster.

I knew that Webster wouldn't be able to keep his big fat mouth shut and would mention my name, hence I'm not there as you well know. You might have my name, if that is my real name, but you still haven't worked out why they all had to die yet. So, it is looking likely that body 16 will be found soon, only who will that body be is the question…

Again, the email address was deleted and was untraceable. One by one, the patrol vehicles returned. No one had seen him. Thomas had no choice but to inform the B team. They were next on duty and doing the night shift. He hadn't wanted to involve them as he hadn't built up the trust with them like he had his own team. He had quite a few arguments with various officers over the years and bridges hadn't been built with some of them since. Time was closing in, so he had no choice.

The day was nearly over, and they still hadn't worked out the reasons why. Thomas was going out of his mind with worry when the phone rang. It was Artis.

'Hello, is that DCI Thomas?'

'Yes, it is, is that Artis?' replied Thomas.

'Yes, Artis here, I think we may have some interesting information for you. Does the name Dumesh mean anything to you?'

'Yes, he is one of the officers in my team, but he hasn't shown up for a few days,' Thomas said.

'Well, the person Boris and his brother Stephan were going to meet was a man called Dumesh. It is alleged that Stephan was the possible biological father of Dumesh and he wanted to meet up with him. Boris had suggested going with him as it could be a crank and they could use the time to do some sightseeing. We found this on Boris' emails as Stephan had emailed him about the possibility of being a father and asking Boris for advice as he had been in England months before this Dumesh had been born. Apparently, Stephan had come over to England for a two-year break and worked day and night doing various jobs and had got himself into some trouble with the police; he was told he could either be deported back to Latvia or go to prison. He chose the first option. Before he had left, he been in a relationship so there was a strong possibility that he was the father.'

'Well, that solves why they were all killed, they all must have gone to meet this Dumesh together, but what about the others, did Stephan put anything else in his emails to his brother that might help us?' Thomas asked earnestly.

'Ah, that's where it gets interesting. He told Boris that he wasn't looking forward to returning to the town he had once lived in as there were people there that he would rather forget about as they weren't nice characters. When Boris had pressed him, he had told him that he had worked in a butcher's shop during the day and it was run by three brothers; they weren't very nice to him, they constantly made fun of him, ridiculing him at every opportunity and they paid him very little. To make ends meet, he worked behind the bar of some pub run by a man called Charles something or other. This Charles had sacked him when he had found out that he was seeing a woman, calling him all the names under the sun, as she was a married woman. Her name was Tracey; he didn't mention any surnames. The rest of the emails is about their flights and political stuff. I hope this helps you,' Artis said.

Thomas thanked him for the information, telling him that he had been most helpful and that he hoped one day they could meet in person so he could personally thank him for his help and hard work.

Thomas went through all this new information in his head and was about to let the team know before they left for the night when the penny dropped. His own mother was called Tracey, and after he had left home to join the force, his parents had suddenly got divorced. His mother had been having an affair with a younger man. His father had found out and threw her out of the house, throwing her belongings into the street after her. He had not seen his mother for years after that. When he did manage to catch up with her, she had managed to get herself a flat by persuading the bank to loan her some money. When she couldn't make the repayments and the bank was demanding the money or they were going to repossess, she got mixed with some lowlife who helped her out financially. Being in the force, Thomas had wiped his hands of her and had walked away, telling himself that his mother was dead to him.

The pieces were starting to fit together.

He fled out of the office as if he was Usain Bolt and shouted to everyone to gather around. As he wrote on the board under each name of the deceased, he spoke:

'Right, I've just had an interesting phone call with Artis he told me that Stephan is the potential father of Dumesh. He had an affair with my bloody mother! He had lived in England for a couple of years. He had worked at a butcher's shop run

44

by three brothers, so that accounts for Joe, John and Jordan. They paid him peanuts and took the micky out of him whenever they could. He also worked behind a bar, but the landlord sacked him when he found out that he was seeing a married woman more than twice his age. So that must be Charlie. Bob must be the banker that helped my mother get a loan to purchase a flat when my father kicked her out and Eddie must be the bloke who helped her out when she fell on hard times… So that just leaves four people unaccounted for, Dave and Trevor, the small-time crooks, and Frank and Warren, the two homeless guys.'

The room was buzzing with this new information.

'So, if Stephan was seeing your mother and she was pregnant, Dumesh could be your half-brother,' someone piped up.

'Yes, that thought had crossed my mind, but when I did see her some years later, she didn't have a child with her, there was no sign of a child ever living with her, either. She could have given the child up for adoption, though,' Thomas declared.

Things were starting to look a bit more hopeful.

He left the office with a glimmer of hope in his heart. He had got the B team to keep looking for Dumesh, and for once they all seemed keen to help out. He went straight to the Chinese takeaway and ordered the set menu for two. He couldn't wait to tell Andrews the latest developments.

As he got to the hotel room, he noticed that there was no police guard, and that the door was slightly ajar. He dropped the bag of food and pushed open the door. There, sitting on the edge of the bed was Andrews. Her hands and feet were tethered with a rope. She had a strip of blue material around her face. She was gagged. Her dazzling blue eyes were wide open with terror and those long eyelashes were moist with the tears.

From the corner Thomas approached the bed and Dumesh came out of the bathroom. He was holding a gun.

'So, aren't you the clever one then,' Dumesh smirked.

'Why, Dumesh, why?' Was all Thomas could utter.

Dumesh laughed and said:

'From birth, I was bought up in various children's homes. I had an awful time, especially with two particular people and I vowed I would get revenge. I did, didn't I? I well and truly did,' he said with satisfaction.

'So, what about all those people and why have you got beef with Andrews or me, come to that matter?' Thomas asked.

'Ah, you will have to wait for the answer to that, I want to first give you credit for finding out about the 11 of them, which under such stress and the circumstances of the added torment from me, was pretty good. A lot of people would have cracked and ran the opposite way after all the sixteens I left behind and the fires. So, I must applaud you.'

Dumesh paused for a while, and then continued:

'When I eventually left the children's home, I managed to get hold of all the documents held on my file. In there, it told me that my mother's name was Tracey Thomas and my father's name was Stephan Dumesh. I was given up shortly after being born. I tracked down Tracey. I didn't tell her who I was obviously. I told her I was doing some research into how women coped in society with it still being dominantly a man's world, and do you know what, the stupid bitch fell for it, hook line and sinker. She told me all about her abusive husband,

46

your father; he was a drunk and a violent man who controlled her. She fell for Stephan in a big way as he made her feel like a princess. Well things took a turn for the worse when he was sacked from his pub job; he couldn't look after himself let alone a woman on what he got paid from the butcher's. That's when he met some crooks and then he was deported back to his homeland. Oh, he could have gone to prison for a spell but my mother, our mother, had gone and secured a flat, so it looked like she didn't need him anymore. She did, however, see him just before he left for Latvia and she told him she was pregnant, but she wasn't sure who the father was, it could have been the two guys at the squat that she had lived in before getting the flat.'

'But if she wasn't sure who the father was, why did she name Stephan on the files as the father?' Thomas asked.

'She had secretly squirreled away some hair samples of all three of them and when the baby was born, me, she got a DNA test done. When she found out the truth, she did write to him, well it was sent to his parent's address as she had remembered it and wrote it down when he was deported. She did get a reply, saying that Stephan had moved on and was happy and didn't want anything to do with her or the baby, so she gave me up. The heartless bitch. She said she felt awful for doing so, but she couldn't afford to raise a child on her own with no job. Once she had dumped me with social services, she turned to drink herself. When I found her, she was in a mess. She wasn't what I was expecting at all. I almost, almost, felt sorry for her. But as you can see, I'm kind of heartless.' With that, he fell into a fit of laughter.

'That still doesn't explain Boris, his wife and their two children, does it?'

'They were just there. I couldn't get Stephan away from them, so they were just collateral damage. Boris might have known about me from the beginning, so I didn't think twice about him anyway. I did feel for his wife and kids though, but they all represented what I didn't have.' Dyke answered.

'So where do we both fit in?' Thomas asked again.

'You are the son of that bitch and she' – he pointed to Andrews – 'declined my advances when I first became part of the team, and it made me feel like that little boy in the children's home all over again every time she looked down her nose at me. I didn't know who I despised the most, her or you, so I have toyed with that decision over and over again.'

All the time they had been talking Dumesh had the gun firmly placed in his hands and was moving it to Andrews and then to Thomas and then back to Andrews. He was playing cat and mouse with them. He was enjoying himself; he had a little audience and could brag about it. He was actually having fun, watching the terror in their eyes and trying to work out which one would be Body 16. Whilst Dumesh had been talking, Thomas had managed to sit next to Andrews and had been fiddling around with the rope. Once he had managed to undo the knots, he signalled to Andrews that when he shouted roll, she was to roll under the bed. Her father had taken a bullet for him, now it was his turn to return the favour. If necessary, he was going to take a bullet for her. Fair was fair in his eyes and he was retiring soon; she still had a whole life ahead of her.

Thomas stood up and shouted roll and made a lunge at Dumesh. Andres rolled over and managed to wriggle under the bed, as she did so the gun went off. Everything went quiet for a while. Then all hell broke loose. People were screaming in the corridors as they heard the gunshot. Andrews managed to untie her feet and remove the gag from around her mouth. She peered through the end of the bed. She could see both men, Thomas and Dumesh, lying on the floor. Andrews scrambled out of her hiding place and went straight over to Thomas. He had been hit. He told her in a whispered tone to get out and get help. The police were already on their way, other hotel guests had already rung them. With hindsight, they had sent paramedics as well.

Police stormed the room and despite still being unconscious, Dumesh was handcuffed.

The paramedics tended to Thomas and whisked him off in the ambulance. Lights and sirens were on to get him to the hospital as quick as possible. All the way there, the paramedics were working constantly on him. He had lost a lot of blood. Andrews had to clambered into the ambulance with him. She had been told that the marks on her wrists and ankles needed to be looked at, for one, and for another, she didn't want Thomas to be on his own. The paramedics had already radioed through to the hospital and a team of nurses and doctors met them at the door. Thomas was soon whisked into the operating theatre. His life was now in their hands. Andrews was seen by another doctor and although her wrists and ankles were sore and bruised, the nurse was told to put on some cream and bandage them up, just to be on the safe side. Afterwards Andrews was left on her own. She paced the corridors and drank numerous cups of coffee offered to her by the nurses. It was the longest five hours of her life. Eventually, he was bought back to the ICU. Once he was there and she knew he had survived the operation, her emotions got the better of her and she cried. She cried for him, cried for herself and cried with relief that this whole nightmare was over.

Andrews walked over to the nurses' station and rang the station to give them the news that Thomas was an out of theatre but was in a critical but stable way. She stayed at the hospital that night and the following day, she only left his side when she had a call of nature or when the nurses and doctors had to tend for him. Eventually after what seemed like days, he was taken off the critical list. He had woken up enough to smile at Andrews and give her a thumbs up.

Andrews took a taxi back to the station and met the desk sergeant at the door, who gladly paid the fare for her. She had left in the ambulance that quick with Thomas that she hadn't had time to grab her purse. As she walked in, everyone got on their feet and cheered, all except one. That's when she realised Dumesh had an accomplice, someone in the team was leaking information to him every time they found something. Webster. Andrews walked up to him and slapped him hard across his face. As he went to rub his face, she grabbed his arm and bend it behind him, before signally to someone to handcuff him. Andrews read him his rights.

It emerged later, when he was questioned that Webster and Dumesh had been in a relationship together. Dumesh had even tried it on with Andrews to try and cover up the fact that he was gay, but she had spurned his advances. He had only done that as Webster was married and was due to become a father any day. Dumesh had used his charm then when that didn't work, he had blackmailed Webster to make him tell him everything about the investigation, what they had found, when and where, he wanted every little detail. Dumesh had showed Webster a video that he had secretly taken of the two of them having sex and said he would share it on the internet, send it to his wife and all of the team. This was enough to make Webster comply with his wishes. He had used a burner phone every time he had called Dumesh and given him the latest updates. He had been hoping to get away with it, but the more things that went on and when Thomas had said did anyone know about anyone with Latvian connections, he had thought it might be a way of getting Dumesh off his back and he could carry on as if nothing had happened.

Andrews sussed him out straight away. Someone must have been telling Dumesh that they had found 11 bodies, then another four. Dumesh knew that they hadn't had any luck on the first three days, so someone must have been letting Dumesh know every step of the way and then when Webster didn't stand with the rest of the team, she knew he was the man, he was the mole, Dumesh's informant.

Thomas made a slow but full recovery. Whilst he was laid up in his hospital bed, he was interviewed about what had happened in the hotel room. He stated everything that Dumesh had said and then told them that when he had shouted roll to Andrews, he had made a lunge towards Dumesh and the gun. As he fell to the ground with Dumesh, the gun had gone off and he had been shot. Dumesh had hit his head on the corner of the dresser, which had knocked him out. Once he had signed his statement, he turned to the officer, who had conducted with interview and said in a whisper:

'It's a good job I was shot as I would have killed him with my bare hands.'

Two weeks later, he was discharged from the hospital. He didn't let anyone know, he wanted to surprise everyone, so he went straight to the station, also, he still didn't have a home to go to because he still hadn't been able to sort his house out after the fire. Unbeknown to him, the team had come together and had gone to his house and done the necessary repairs, repainted the kitchen and front room and replaced some of the items for him. Andrews had snuck his key out of the hospital bedside locker whilst he was sleeping and had replaced it the following day after she had one cut. The team were there. When they clapped eyes on him, they all stood up and cheered and clapped. He was a hero in everyone's eyes but none more than Andrews. She owed him her life. Once everyone had stopped cheering, asking him how he was feeling, given him the update on Webster being arrested as Dumesh informant and how Andrews had slapped him hard across his face, they told him about what they had been doing to his house in his absence. Thomas was overcome with emotion that his team would do that for him that tears actually sprang to his eyes. He was so grateful to them. He hadn't been looking forward to staying at a hotel again, in fact he didn't ever want to stay in another hotel for the rest of his life.

It took another few weeks for all the paperwork to be completed ready for the trial. Dumesh had been given medical attention for his concussion and cut to his head and then had been taken straight to the police station.

Once there, he was read his rights again. They had wanted to make sure that there could be no loopholes that an eagle eyed, jumpstart barrister could find. So, the Miranda was the first thing they did and even recorded it so even though they had read it at the scene and at the station, it was on tape and no one could say they hadn't read it to him.

DCI Thomas had decided to put his retirement on hold until after the trial. This had been personal, and he owed it to the team, they had made a fantastic job of his house.

Although he had fallen out with his mother years ago, it was still his mother at the end of the day and to think Dumesh was his half-brother. That thought made him want to vomit every time he let his mind think about it. He wanted to kill Dumesh with his bare hands, and he said that if he were in a different profession, he just might carry that out. The only thing that stopped him was that he had an exemplary record, and he didn't want to ruin that. He couldn't let scum like him take away everything he worked hard to achieve. He was better than that.

He didn't do any of the interviews, he couldn't actually trust himself to not jump across the table and pummel his face in. Andrews had wanted to be part of the interviews, but it was deemed best not to let her do them as after all, he had tried to proposition her and had targeted her. Two guys from CID performed the interviews as all the team were too closely involved, and with Dumesh and Webster being part of that team, it was deemed inappropriate. What they had done was set up the room next door so that Thomas, Andrews and anyone else could listen in to what was being said. Singh and Jackson took over.

'For the purpose of the tape in the room are CID Singh and CID Jackson, the accused Stephen Dumesh. The time is 9:05 am precisely,' Singh said.

'You know why you have been arrested and are here, don't you?' Singh continued.

'Yes.'

'Before we start, can you confirm that you have refused to have a solicitor present,' Jackson butted in.

'Yes,' repeated Dumesh.

'How to you plead to each murder? All 15 of them?' Singh asked.

'Guilty to each and every one,' Dumesh said, with an air of arrogance.

'How do you plead with the kidnap and restraining of a police officer?'

'Guilty.'

'How do you plead with bribing a police office?' Jackson pressed.

'Not guilty, he owed me, and I cashed in,' sneered Dumesh.

'Let's start at the beginning, shall we? Let's talk about your childhood a little, so we can get the full picture of you as a person.'

Dumesh sat back in his chair and relaxed; he was liking this, he felt important. He wanted to be famous and this was his chance.

'Like I said to Thomas and Andrews, I was bought up in many children's homes after that bitch of a mother gave me up. It was whilst I was in one of them that I met Dave and Trevor. At first, they took me under their wing as they were a couple of years older than me. After a while, the bullying started. When anything happened, I was the brunt of their aggression, and if they did anything wrong, they would automatically blame me, so I got the beating from the staff. It became the norm. After a couple of years of this abuse and torment, I ran away. I was classed as a troublesome kid and put into a secure unit. It was whilst I was in there that I made up my mind of getting them back and making them pay for what they put me through. That consumed me every day, every minute of the day, to be precise. I'd even dream about it,' laughed Dumesh.

It was a sinister laugh that made Singh and Jackson look at each other as if to say, *We have a psychopath here*.

'Go on,' Jackson eventually said, when Dumesh had finished laughing.

'When I became too old to stay in the unit and they finally let me out, I managed to get hold of the file that social services had on me. It named my biological mother and father. It had said that he had returned to his native country, Latvia, so I concentrated on finding her. I was intrigued to find out why she had given me up, I was also angry as to why she abandoned me, because her decision to hand me over to social services didn't give me the best start in life, now did it? Plus, every beating I had received, I wanted to do to her, see how she felt.'

'So, did you find her?' inquired Singh.

'Yes. I managed to track her down, took me a while, though. I turned up on her doorstep and told her a story that I was doing some research into how women cope in a man's world and someone had given me her name and address. She gladly let me in. She wasn't what I was expected, though, to be honest. She was a frail, grey haired little old lady. She looked much older than her actual age. She told me that I had better get all the information I needed quickly as she hadn't got much longer left, she was dying. Dying with cancer. She was riddled with it; I was there about four hours in all. Every so often, she would take a break to either get her breath back or to take some more pain relief. This made me happy, to be

honest with you. She was suffering and not by my hands.'
Dumesh laughed.

'Well, she went on to explain that she had married young and had a son, David, not long afterwards. Everything was fine until her husband lost his job and had turned to drink, which in turn had made him violent. She said that she had done what she could for David but with hardly any money, they both went without many times. As David got older, he too was at the mercy of his dad's beatings and that bitch said she sat and watched. She didn't intervene, she just shrugged it off when I asked her why not, and said that whilst he was beating David, he was leaving her alone. I nearly choked on my cup of tea, I'll tell you. I couldn't believe that a mother would or could say that about her own child. But she said all right, said it as if it was a natural thing to do. I was beginning to think that maybe I had been the lucky one not being bought up by her. Anyway, enough about what I was thinking. She said that she met this Stephan guy, who worked at the butcher's. He would often slip in a bit extra meat when the brothers had their backs turned. He had taken a shine to her and had often seen her with bruises and rummaging around in her bag for coppers to pay the bill. He had wanted to protect her. Well, to cut a long story short, they began an affair. The brothers still picked on him relentlessly but having her in his life made it bearable. He didn't make much money there, so he started to work behind the bar, which was enough to keep him going. He hadn't known that the landlord was a good friend of her husband until he had sacked him on the spot when he had bought her into work one day. The landlord was a Charles something, the locals often called him Charlie. Apparently, he was a law-abiding citizen, well that's what she said, and didn't want any trouble. He had inherited the pub from his late father and had worked hard to make it a success. There was a recession on, and he didn't want gossip mongers ruining his reputation and staying away from his pub. He didn't care about who or what his customers were, as long as they spent their money there. He'd welcome mass murderers there if they had money to spend, she said. Maybe I could go and have a pint or two there,' Dumesh said, bursting into a fit of laughter.

Singh and Jackson wanted to suspend the interview when Dumesh said he wanted to continue. It was clear to the two of them that he was enjoying himself. He was relishing in this.

'The level of abuse she had suffered reminded me of what I had been through. It made me angry. When Charlie told her husband, he had gone mad and that was when she was thrown out onto the streets. He even threw her belongings into the street to make her feel humiliated. Once Charlie had sacked him Stephan wasn't able to make enough money to keep them both. He hardly made enough to support himself, let alone her as well. That was when he met two lads, Dave and Trevor. They wanted him to do some errands for them. When they told him what they would pay him, he jumped at the chance. He loved her and would do anything for her. Even if it was dodgy and breaking the law, he didn't care. He'd even die for her, which is a bit ironic now, isn't it? He did! Well eventually, he was nicked, and he was faced with either being deported or going to prison for a spell. He couldn't stand the thought of being locked up, as he had just spent a month on remand and had hated it, so he chose to be deported. He had been hoping that she would go to Latvia with him, but she had told him that she couldn't leave her beloved son behind. So now you see why I targeted Thomas; if it hadn't been for him, she might have gone to Latvia with him and my life would have been completely different. When I found out that he was in the police force, I joined up and did my training. I made sure that once I had graduated and had some experience, I got a transfer to his division. I did use another name though but a big mistake on my part was that I told Webster my real surname was Dumesh. I had fallen in love with him, and I thought he loved me too; that was until I found out he was married with a child on the way.'

'Why did you use a different surname?' Jackson inquired.

'Well, you know how it is, anything different about you, people pick on you for, I thought having a foreign name would make me a target for more bullying and I'd had enough of that during my childhood.'

Dumesh took a sip of the bottle of water that he had been given and sat back in his chair. He was so relaxed anybody who was looking in would think he was telling a story rather than confessing to the heinous crimes he had committed.

'I digress, let me carry on,' he almost pleaded.

'She had told him that she was pregnant but that she wasn't sure who the father was. Apparently when she was first kicked out by her abusive husband, she had lived in a squat with these two men. She had been made to have sex with them to ensure that she could stay there. She said it was better than sleeping on the streets, the slut. Stephan was enraged and had gone to Latvia with a heavy broken heart. She wrote to him after I was born, telling him that she had had a DNA test to prove the paternity of her son and he was the father but the reply that came back wasn't what she was expecting. His mother had written to her, saying he had moved on, was happy and wanted nothing more to do with her or her illegitimate son. She said she had little money and felt that it was in her son's best interest to give him up. He would have all the things that she couldn't give him. Well, that was wrong, wasn't it?' He smirked.

'She went on to say that he was a beautiful baby. He had a mop of blond curly hair and big blue eyes and she was sure that when an adoptive family saw him, they would fall in love with him, it would be love at first sight and give him the life she couldn't. I had the look of an angel. Well, that is what is written in my files and that was the reason why she had given me up. An angel, eh, would they still call me that now, or the devil?' he retorted with a real air of arrogance.

All that Jackson could say was, "Probably."

Dumesh laughed again at his own sort of joke. His laugh was getting on Jackson's and Singh's nerves.

'When the bitch got rid of me, I suppose she was feeling guilty, she turned to drink. She had already been to the bank when she was pregnant with me and had managed to secure a mortgage on a little flat. When she fell on hard times again because of her heavy drinking, she met this man, Eddie. He needed somewhere to stash his haul of drugs and for someone to cut it, bag it and sell it. He had already done a few stints in prison for armed robbery and drug offences and didn't want to ever go back in there, so he needed somewhere to do his dirty work as he knew he would be the first to get raided if word got out that there was still cocaine being sold in the area. For doing that he paid a good price, and she was able to pay her bills. It had been a Godsend to her at the time. He had threatened her, and she was terrified of him so she did everything he asked of her, he was well aware that if she did get raided, then she wouldn't mention his name, he had made sure of that fact. I could tell she was still scared of him; you could see it in her eyes when she spoke about him. I suppose I did feel a little sorry for her then, only a little bit, though, I may add. She had, after all, ruined my life, so I was kind of glad she hadn't had the best of times. She had given it all up after Eddie got a bad batch of cocaine and had her cut it with another substance. A handful of people had died, and a few were hospitalised because of it. She sold her flat and moved out of the area. That's when I found her, she had only relocated about eight months prior. She knew she was dying and wanted to live her last few months in peace. I thanked her for her time and left her to it. I could see that she hadn't got long left, may be a day or so at the most. She had no friends or family; she was completely on her own. That was enough justice for me, she would die a lonely woman. As I left, I vowed I would get even with Eddie, I now knew that it was because of his dodgy drugs that the only person that I truly loved, more than I ever did with Webster, had died. He had killed him with those drugs. He had been to a rave with some other friends and had snorted some cocaine with them. It was the first and last time that he ever took drugs. He died a day later in hospital. I was heartbroken, as you can imagine. By joining the force, I was able to access the data base to find out where all the low lives lived so I could watch them from a distance. On the day before the storm started, I hired a van. I covered the windows with black tape and set about my business.'

With that, Dumesh sat right back in his chair and sighed. He was quiet for a moment whilst he remembered everything that he had done that day. Jackson and Singh decided to have a break. They both needed a coffee and something to eat, and they were sure that Dumesh would need some refreshments; he had only had a few sips from his water. They got someone to take him back to cell after saying into the tape the time and that the interview was suspended to have a toilet and refreshment break.

A duty solicitor had been listening in and had asked to see Dumesh. He tried to persuade him to plead insanity, but Dumesh told him he was not needed, and he wasn't going to plead insanity, he was of sound mind. In fact, he told the solicitor that he was proud of the fact that he got rid of the reprobates. He wanted to tell his story.

DCI Thomas had been listening into the interview for the entire time. He had been shocked to hear that his mother was dying from cancer and that she was all alone. He felt torn, should he find her and go and see her before it was too late out of a sense of duty or should he leave her like she had left him to take the beatings from his father. He could clearly remember the beatings he had received from him and the severity of some of them. He could clearly see his mother sitting there, watching it all and then trying to comfort him afterwards. Andrews, who was also present, could sense what he was thinking and put her hand on his arm, and said:

'I know you'll make the right decision.'

With that, she got up and left to fetch them a coffee.

An hour later, Jackson and Singh were ready to resume the interview. Dumesh had requested that he wanted this interview to continue; he wanted it out the way. This time, Dumesh let the duty solicitor in to join them, not to help him to get off the murder charges; those he was proud of, but he didn't want to be charged with bribing Webster. Webster had deserved everything he got; if he hadn't lied to him in the first place about being married and pretending to be gay, then he wouldn't have been involved, so it was his own fault.

Singh spoke into the tape.

'Interview commencing at 1:46 pm, CID Singh, CID Jackson, Stephen Dumesh and Mr Adam Watts present.

'Can you tell me what happened the morning you hired the van?' asked Singh.

Dumesh leaned forward, putting his elbows on the table and smiled.

'Certainly,' he said proudly.

'First, I taped up the windows like I have already told you, then loaded the van with rope, strips of material ready for gags, I had really thought this through what I would need. I was on a high when I drove off. I headed straight to the butchers. Joe was outside in the backyard behind the shop, putting the rubbish into the big bins. I just pointed my gun at his head and ordered him to walk to my van. I made him climb into the back, and once he was there, I punched him hard in the side of his head, knocking him out. It was as easy as that. Then I tied his hands and feet together and gagged him. I dragged him to the front of the van so there was room for others. Clever, eh?' Dumesh said and waited a while before he continued.

'If you think I am going to tell you that it was clever, then you are mistaken, Dumesh, please go on,' Jackson said through gritted teeth. Dumesh was getting to him; you could see how much pleasure he was getting from relaying what he had done. He was one sick man. It was taking all of Jackson's strength and professionalism not to get up and wipe the ugly smile of his face.

'I went back to the yard behind the shop again. Jordan came out calling for Joe, so I just did the exact same to him. This was getting easy; I was getting a right buzz from it, I'll tell you. I went back for the third time, hoping that John would come out looking for his brothers, but he was too busy setting up the shop for the day's business. I had to go in and find him, saying that I had heard moaning as if someone was hurt badly and he needed to come with me. He had looked at me quizzically, so I told him I was from the shop next door and I had only just started working there. John believed me, the fool. That's when I grabbed him. With all three safely tied up and gagged, I drove to Charlie's pub. It was not open to the public yet, as it was too early in the morning, but he was expecting deliveries. Every Thursday morning, he had his deliveries ready for the rush of the weekend. He wasn't going to get one, though, this Thursday, not that he knew that at the time. I had already rung the brewery, cancelling them due to some hospital appointment. So, when I knocked on his door, he must have just presumed I was the delivery guy. He was big built, so I had to use all my strength to knock him out. As I have said before, I had been watching these people for a while so I knew that a punch to the side of his head wouldn't have floored him, so I used my baseball bat instead. The worse thing about that was then I had to drag the fat useless lump of lard to the van. He started to stir as I tried to haul him inside, so I pointed my gun at his temple and told him to get in. As he scrambled into the van, I hit him again across the back of his head. He fell headfirst onto the van floor. I was then able to tie him up and gag him. The adrenaline was pumping now through my body and I easily dragged him to the front and plonk him with the other three.' Dumesh paused again, smiling as he remembered every detail.

Then he continued, 'As I drove along, all four started to stir and come around. That's when I started to talk to them. I told them that their actions had ruined a man's life and that I was going ruin theirs. They all looked bewildered and confused so I said, you three idiots, Joe, Jordan and John, you weren't nice employers, were you? If you hadn't been so cruel to one particular person and had paid him a decent wage, then he wouldn't have had to work in a pub to make ends meet. You all picked on him because he was foreign, you nasty pieces of shit. I could tell that they realised who I was on about after they had thought about it. You, Charlie, if you cared more about the customers who came into your boozer and not just the money they were spending, then you would have decent clientele and then you wouldn't have to sack your bar staff, sacking someone for having an affair with someone is out of order, it had nothing to do with you. Okay, you might have known her husband, but did you know he was beating her and their son almost daily. I bet you didn't know that, did you? But because he spent a lot of money most days, you wanted his custom to continue so you got rid of the one person who could have saved her and the child. You have no morals, yet you try and say you are an honourable person with high standards. You are just a greedy man. You are all to blame in your own ways. I could see the sheer look of terror in their eyes through the rear-view mirror, as by now they had shuffled up and were sitting huddled together. It was quite a sad sight to be fair. Four grown up men that had been ruthless now, sitting there terrified. They were now 25 years older; Charlie was now 46 years old and the others were 49, 51 and

53 years old. No matter how hard they squirmed about, they couldn't untie the knots, I had made sure that even if they managed to get together, they wouldn't be able to untie each other. I suppose that's one thing I can thank the boy scouts for, teaching me about knots.' He laughed his sinister laugh again.

The solicitor wanted to have a break, but Dumesh insisted that he carried on. He was enjoying himself too much. He was getting a right thrill, looking at the faces of Jackson and Singh as he was explaining what had happened that day.

'Next was Eddie. I'd been watching him for a while and I knew that every Thursday at ten o'clock, he went to this particular house and I smiled to myself as I drove there as I knew he wouldn't be going in there that day. He was an easy target. He was now in his 50s and due to all the drugs he had taken throughout his life it had taken a toll on his health, anyone could see that. As he got out his car, I struck. All I had to do was tell him I had got his name from an associate and that he might be interested in seeing what I had to offer. I told him I had a case full of drugs in my van and the street value was worth thousands of pounds and that he could purchase the lot from me for a reasonable price. I would cut him a good deal if he wanted them and that I would do business with him on a regular basis. I knew he would fall for it, he was greedy, he wanted to make his fortune, but he also wanted drugs for his own use. He followed me straight away to the van, idling, talking on the way. Once I opened the door, it was wham, I struck him hard. I knocked the little weed out straight away. I then tied and gagged him. I decided that once I had put his gag on that I would break his nose. So, I did. He would find breathing hard just like my boyfriend had when he had been hooked to a life support machine, the ventilator breathing on his behalf. This was getting easier and better than any drug on the streets. Dave and Trevor were next on my list. I had already sent them a bogus letter, saying that I was from the council and was coming to inspect their house. If they refused to let me in, then their housing benefit could be suspended, and they could end up being evicted. They must have fell for my letter, as both the idiots were in and waiting for me. I had a clipboard with me and went around the house as if I were a real council official. They definitely weren't gentlemen as when we went down the stairs after checking the bedrooms, they went first, kinda rude, don't you think? That's when I decided to act. I shoved the one in front of me that hard that he fell straight into his mate and they both toppled down the stairs. It was a funny sight, to be honest, and I had to laugh. I quickly ran down after them and tied them up before they had change to get to their feet. They were hurt from their falls and at first refused to get up, Dave had badly twisted his foot, so hopping was out of the question for him. Once I pointed my gun at them, they both struggled to stand and Trevor immediately hopped on the van, I had to help Dave, though. I had parked the van on the drive. I had reversed onto the drive and the back door of the van was right outside their front door, so I was being thoughtful, they didn't have far to hop. The house was in a quiet cul-de-sac and I had done my research beforehand and knew the other residents were at work. I had nothing to fear, no one would see or hear anything unusual. By half past eleven, I had seven of them. I was ahead of schedule.' He smiled again, thinking of his achievements so far, he was as pleased as punch with himself.

They decided to leave it there and would resume the next morning. Dumesh was getting tired and neither Jackson nor Singh wanted the duty solicitor to say that they had coerced a confession out of him because he was exhausted so had confessed just to get out of there.

Thomas was still in a quandary about what to do when Andrews slipped a piece of paper under his hand. It was Tracey Thomas' address.

Thomas looked at it over and over again debating, *Shall I go or not?* He even deliberated on tossing a coin; *Heads I go, tails I don't*, he thought.

Andrews broke his thoughts by saying softly:

'Do what you heart says, you might even be too late. She might have already died, after all this was weeks ago and he said she only had days to live, but according to the department of health, her pension and benefits are still being collected. I know you, you will need to ask her those questions such as why, so you can move on. I can see that clearly etched on your face.'

Thomas nodded and thanked her. He went to his car and typed in the address into his sat nav. It was about an hour's drive away but it had taken longer due to the rush hour traffic. All the time questions he wanted to ask went through his mind. A couple of times he nearly turned around to go back home but he persisted with the traffic and eventually arrived at his destination. He turned off the engine and looked at the house. It was a small, terraced house. The tiny little garden at the front was just slabbed, no flowers, just grey concrete. He was nervous as he knocked the door. He didn't know whether she was dead or alive, if she would recognise him or even if she would want to talk to him, after all, he had turned his back on her and hadn't spoken to her in years, over 20, to be precise. He waited patiently until after a good few minutes, a frail woman opened the door. As their eyes met, she smiled and instantly cried. She could not believe her eyes; her son had come to visit, he was standing in front of her. She beckoned him in. She shuffled to her armchair and asked him to sit down too. Thomas cleared his throat and asked her about when he was a child and why she hadn't jumped in when his father was beating him. She looked directly at him and through her tears she managed to say:

'David, I am so sorry for not protecting you when you were younger, you must have thought I was a right monster, a really bad mother. Your dad had already threatened me, saying that whenever he beat you, I had to watch, if I tried to stop him or shield you, then he would break your bones or even kill you. I was terrified, I knew he was capable of doing that to you. He knew how much you meant to me, so he punished me by torturing you. So you see, I had no choice in the matter. It was a case of watching or seeing you get broken bones or being killed by his bare hands. That's when I met this man, Stephan. He made me feel human again. Your dad had ruined my self-esteem but he helped to restore it. Your dad found out and threw me into the streets. He had heard from Charlie that he had already sacked him, your dad must have kept an eye on what we did as it was him who dobbed Stephan into the police when he got involved with crime, he only did it to provide for us.' She paused to wipe her nose and wipe her tears. She needed to catch her breath too. This was the most she had talked to anyone in weeks. She turned her oxygen on and sat for a few minutes until she felt she could continue.

'I had another son, your brother, but I had to give him up as I had no money and no job to support him. I didn't tell you before as I was ashamed of myself and I knew you were ashamed of me and I couldn't bear the fact of you hating me more than you already did. After all, I hardly saw you after your dad chucked me out.' She coughed and hacked into her pile of tissues. The tears fell down her cheeks, soaking her top.

Thomas said gently, 'Why didn't you come to me for help, instead of getting involved with Eddie and drugs?'

'I had already made a mess of my life and I knew I had helped mess up your childhood as I hadn't saved you from the hands of your dad, you were just starting out in the force and doing well, I didn't want to mess that up for you as well.'

'Oh, Mum,' Thomas managed to utter. It was the first time he had uttered the word "mum" in years and it had felt good. He flung his arms around her tiny frail body. He could feel every bone sticking out her near translucent skin. She had never been a big woman anyway, but the weight she had lost was making her almost skeletal.

They both apologised and forgave each other and cried together. They cried for the lost time between them. Tracey looked up at Thomas, and said:

'Thank you for coming to see me, my darling David, I love you so very much, I never stopped loving you.'

She smiled; it was a real smile, the first proper meaningful smile that she had done for years. She kissed his hands and lay her head back to rest. Thomas sat on the floor in front of her and lay his head on her lap. She gently caressed his hair like she had done when he was a small boy.

A whole lot of emotions flowed through him, which he was coming to terms with as each one ran through him when all of a sudden, she stopped stroking his hair. Her hand was still resting on top of his head, but her hand wasn't moving at all. He carefully sat up removing her hand gently so he could check for a pulse. She was gone.

He made some calls and waited for the undertakers to come and collect her body. The doctor had already been out and signed her death certificate.

He took the time he waited for them to arrive to have a look around her home. She hadn't got many possessions, no ornaments on show and no pictures on the walls. In the cupboard of the dresser was a photograph album. It was filled with pictures of Thomas as a baby and a young boy. The pictures went up until he was twelve years old. On a few of the pictures, he could see a faint outline of bruises on his body and he flinched at the sight of them. The pages were well worn as if they had been turned hundreds of times. As he thumbed through the pages, he remembered this woman coming to his house to see his father, it was about a month after he had kicked his mum out, she must have taken the album with her as he had vague memories of it being on the bookcase. It had never dawned on him that it had gone. Next, he found a manila folder. Inside were a couple of photographs of Stephan and her, a couple of the pictures must have been taken whilst she was still with her husband, as you could clearly see bruises over her arms. There was another photograph, small in size. It was a picture of a baby, with curly blond hair and piercing blue eyes. On the back it said "Stephen, son of Stephan", then there was a date, "16th October". Thomas put everything back into the folder. When the undertakers left, he went home. He took the folder and album with him. He rang Andrews and thanked her for giving him that push. She drove around to his with some food as she knew he wouldn't have bothered to stop to get anything to eat. As they ate, he told her all about his visit and how he wished that things could have been different. Andrews asked him what life was like after his mum had left and did his father continue to behave in the same way. Thomas turned to her and said:

'It was extraordinary, to be honest. As soon as Mum had gone, he changed overnight. It was almost instant. He stopped drinking and became a model father. The amount of drinking he had done over those years took its toll and he died because of it when I was 21. I'd only been in the force a few years when I got a call to get to the hospital to say my goodbyes as he was almost dead.'

They finished their food and spoke about Dumesh.

'I can't believe that someone who looked so angelic as a baby could turn out so evil. Here, take a look at the picture of him as a new-born,' he said, handing her the picture from the folder.

'I see what you mean, he was an adorable baby, and you could understand that she thought he would be adopted straight away,' Andrews said, breaking the silence that had come between them.

'I can't get my head around the fact that I was related to him, that he was my half-brother,' Thomas shuddered at this thought.

They spent the rest of the evening taking about the interview and what Dumesh had said about each person so far and the fact that he was getting off on relaying his story. He was definitely a glory seeker. When Andrews finally got up to leave, Thomas thanked her for getting the address of his mother; without that he would have been too late, he would never have got to see her again. She told him that he was welcome. They hugged and said goodnight. They had another long day ahead of them tomorrow, hearing the rest of Dumesh's confession. They were both tired and needed some sleep before they had to sit in the room and listen for hours on end.

At nine o'clock sharp, the interview of Dumesh was about to resume. Andrews and Thomas were already sitting in the adjacent room. The speakers had been tested to make sure they were working.

Once again, Singh spoke into the tape, first introducing the people in the room and then the date and time.

He recapped for Dumesh's sake what he had already told them and asked him if he was ready to continue from where he left off.

Dumesh cleared his throat and sat upright, as if he were about to address on audience on the stage rather than give a police interview.

'Ah, let me think, the next two, Frank and Warren, were even easier. They were still living in a squat and did whatever they wanted to get by. Neither of them had ever had a fixed abode. When I pulled up in my van, telling them that I had a van full of electrical goods that I just needed to get rid of and that they could keep any profits, they jumped at the prospect of making a few pounds and eagerly came to the van to have a look. Once they got there, I opened the doors and shoved my gun hard into the back of one of them and hit the other by slamming the door into him. In a flash, I had bound and gagged them both too. I was soon off on my travels again. I was going to meet my father at long last. They had rented a cottage in a remote part of the country. The house was standalone, there were no other houses around for miles. I needed plenty of time to locate it, as it was down some right country lanes. The people in the back were being right bumped about going down some of them lanes. I couldn't help but laugh as every so often I heard moans and groans coming from them all. I was excited. I had heard great things about him. When I had tracked him down in Latvia, he hadn't rebuked me, he actually wanted to see me. He hadn't written back to Tracey all them years ago, it must have been his mother who had, he said he hadn't heard from her since the day he left England. I parked up and was met at the door by a hard-faced woman, who I later found out was Boris' wife. My excitement of finally meeting my father was short lived, that stupid brother of his Boris joined him. In fact, Boris did most of the talking and wouldn't let Stephan talk for himself. He hardly got a word in. Boris was more bothered about a scandal affecting his political career than Stephan meeting his long-lost son. I'm afraid to say I lost it. I lost it when his mouthy wife told me to crawl back into the hole that I had come from. Boris had laughed at this and that was when I marched up to him and whacked him with all my strength, knocking him clean out. She then came at me with hands flailing at me. I had no choice but to whack her too. She was about to scratch my face off with those perfectly manicured nails of hers. They were more like claws than nails. The two kids were screaming. I soon shut the brats up though when I pointed my gun at them. The room suddenly fell silent and that whim of a man that was supposed to be my father stood there, stock still, I don't know if it was shock or what, but he didn't utter a word other than to open and close his mouth. He didn't take his eyes off me though. Eventually, he found his voice and kept uttering, "I'm sorry, I'm sorry," over and over again. It was getting on my nerves, if truth be told. I ended up shouting at him, "Sorry, sorry, you don't know how sorry you're going to be." This wasn't the reunion that I had in mind. I had got the other people bound and gagged in my van for him. To show him that everything he had been through in England had been taken care of. Now this was all in vain. He wasn't the man I was hoping to meet. Soon, I had all five of them bound and gagged and had them bundled into the back of the van with the others. What a day's work! I had got the 10 I wanted, Joe, Jordan, John, Charlie, Eddie, Dave, Trevor, Frank, and now Stephan. I only wanted Stephan to come with me to see what I was going to do to the others and make them apologise and grovel to him, but that didn't happen, did it? I hadn't planned for 15, I hadn't planned for Boris, Marianna, Tomsk and Martyna. They shouldn't have been there. I didn't know that they were coming with him. Killing them children would upset me I knew that but they had to go. They had seen my face, for a start, and for another thing, I was about to kill their parents, the nasty awful things they were, and I didn't want them to grow up in children's homes like I had. Now, I had 15 people to get rid of. I don't like odd numbers, they spook me, that's when I thought, right I will get Thomas or possibly Andrews. To be honest, I was gunning more for Thomas; he had already had a good life and was the son of that bitch, and if Andrews did manage to solve things, she would get a promotion, but then I thought well, Andrews did turn me down when I propositioned her and if I go for her, then Thomas would have another death in their family on his hands. Her and her dad would be on his conscience for the rest of his born days. So, I was toying with both of them. I wasn't sure which to go for to be honest, but it had to be one of them.'

Dumesh said the latter so casually that it was heard to digest.

Andrews and Thomas looked at each other. They could have been one of his victims. Neither of them knew which one it would have been. It was a terrifying thought to finally hear it. They knew they were being targeted by all the events they had endured but to finally hear it in black and white was hard to hear.

'So, what did you do once they were all in the van?' Thomas and Andrews heard Jackson say over the speakers.

'Well, at first, when I first started out, I wasn't going to kill anyone, I wanted to hurt them, I wanted to scare them, I wanted them to know how I had felt as a boy because of them. But it had got out of hand. I wasn't sure what I was going to do with them, well, I knew about four of them, Boris and his wife, they had directly dissed me and the brats I've already said they would have to go to save them from the horrors of being bought up in care. I drove to a disused warehouse on the outskirts of town. I just drove straight in there, it wasn't locked up or anything, the vandals had seen to that. One by one, I hauled them out. It was exhausting work, Charlie was the worst one, he was heavy, big boned man he was, all that free drink too, he had a right beer belly on him. In the end, I left him in the van. I'd deal with him later, or so I thought, but do you know what? The bastard managed to bring his legs up and booted me straight in the stomach. It knocked me off my feet for a moment and had winded me too. That's when I decided they all had to die. I was going to kill each and every one of them. The anger that had welled up inside of me; I was like a volcano waiting to explode. I cocked my gun, ready to start then the storm started. It was the loudest storm I have ever heard, so that helped me out immensely. Each time the thunder roared, I fired the gun; the thunder muffled all the shots I fired. Clever, eh?' Dumesh smiled as if he were a genius explaining his theory over something new and interesting.

'So, did you shoot all of them?' Singh asked.

'Yes, I did. Yes, I bloody did. I shot the two brats first. They were still snivelling and whimpering. The noise was doing my head in. I did it quick like, bang, bang and then there were 13. I said a little prayer over the two kids. I'm not completely heartless,' he retorted.

'Was there a particular order in who you shot next?' asked Jackson.

'No, the rest were all random, whoever was the nearest to be honest. Well, except Charlie. I shot him straight after the kids. I waited a while after killing him, I was looking at what I had already done and was on a massive high looking at the others and seeing the terror in their faces. Then I just opened fire and shot each one of them. I sat down for a while and rested. I was starting to feel tired. I knew that I would have to dispose of the bodies, so I needed to regain some strength so I could throw them all back into the van and move them.'

'Did they all die instantly?' inquired Singh.

'Yes, they did, you know that from the autopsies that they were shot through the forehead. I carried the bodies back into the van and then collected all the bullets and casings. I had to move the van to retrieve the bullet that I had shot Charlie with. It had gone straight through his head and the van floor and onto the concrete below. I didn't need to wash away any of the blood that had pooled on the warehouse floor. The rain was already doing that for me. Part of the roof was missing, and the rain was now coming in real fast. So, it would have been a waste of precious time to clean that up as well,' he said, pleased with himself that he had thought of everything to hopefully get away with it.

'What did you do next?' Singh pushed.

'You know what I did with them?' Dumesh sneered.

'We need you for the purpose of the tape to tell us in your own words what you did with them afterwards,' Singh said, as calmly as he could muster.

'Well put like that then, how can I resist?' Dumesh laughed again.

The two officers were getting hot under the collar now. They had had enough of his gloating ways. He was nothing more than a monster.

'He thinks he's some sort of God, a hero,' Thomas snarled out loud.

'Shh,' said Andrews, 'let us hear what he has to say.'

'I drove to the river. I thought to myself, any minute now it is going to burst its banks. The rain was torrential, so I knew it wouldn't be long. I had to act fast. The kids and the mouthy bitch of a wife of Boris I weighted down with bricks. I thought the river would be deeper than that and that they would sink to the bottom. The others I dug graves and put the bodies in and covered them back up. I drove off as quick as I could. I didn't want to be caught out when the river overflowed. I took the van to the next city, found a country lane that was deserted and set it alight. Once I got back to mine, I reported it stolen. What I hadn't banked on, sorry for the pun, was the force of the water when the river did burst its banks. The surge of water moved the freshly dug earth that covered the bodies and the three I had thrown in got stuck in the bulrushes and hadn't sunk. The powerful undercurrents of the river when it did overflow must have moved them into the side of the river and then they got tangled up.' Dumesh sighed at this.

'How did you feel when it was radioed in about a body being found by the river?' Jackson asked.

'At first, I panicked, I made some excuse to leave, saying I was feeling unwell. That's when I collared Webster to keep me informed. Then I thought about my fear of odd numbers and my mind went back to Thomas and Andrews. So, I decided to play a game with them whilst I made up my mind who I was going to kill. As I've said. Originally, I wasn't going to kill anyone, it was only meant to be 10 people I went after. Nine people to scare and one to watch whilst I scared the others and made them grovel. I wanted revenge. Revenge for Stephan and me. But that coward Stephan changed all that by bringing his brother and his family. If only he had come on his own. So, it got me thinking. 10 is the number of the month I was born in and 16 is the day I was born on. I've told you I don't like odd numbers, so I started playing my game. That's when I got hold of Andrews' home number; she had left it on a piece of paper in Thomas' office and I got Webster to send it me. A few days before all of this, a few of us had been talking about zodiac signs, she had asked me when my birthday was, so I thought she might make the connection. Some detective she might turn out to be!' Dumesh spat.

'So why did you burn Thomas' house and Andrew's apartment?' asked Jackson.

'Well, they were being so slow about solving things and giving their orders around the station that I wanted to give them a kick up the arse. Or if I was lucky, I could have killed one of them and then I could stop playing games. I was getting tired. But both of them survived the fires, so that didn't work.'

'Is that why you kept leaving the number 16 everywhere?'

'Yes, apart from it being my lucky number, it was all part of the game, I wanted them to be afraid, they had such a good bond together, it was like watching a father and daughter rather than two work colleagues. It made me sick. I wanted to destroy the relationship they had between them. I suppose you could say I was jealous,' he added.

'So, if you don't like odd numbers, why did you say that they had five days to solve it?' Singh said, finally finding his voice.

'Saying five days was really getting to me, I regretted saying that as soon as I had said it. That's why on the fourth day, I had to act. That's when I broke into the hotel room and tied Andrews up and waited till Thomas arrived. I still hadn't at that time decided who I was going to kill and who I was going to let live.' Dumesh took a long pause, then said, 'When Thomas went for me, my hand was on the trigger. I knew that I had shot him when we both went crashing to the floor. I had my 16th victim. I wasn't to know until days later that he had managed to survive.'

'What about Webster? How did you manage to get him on side and report everything to you?' Singh asked.

'Well, you know that he is married and at the time expecting his first child. Well, we had a brief affair when I was a cadet. I had only just started my training and he was one of the instructors that came to teach us. Secretly, I had taken videos of us together of our, shall I say rendezvous with each other. I told him that if he didn't give me up-to-date reports as soon as they happened, then I would leak those videos to his wife and the whole of the force. I showed him a preview, so he knew that I wasn't messing about. His face fell when I showed him them, I just laughed at him. I told him it was my way of hurting him, he knew I had been falling for him, he had been the first person I had let into my life since losing my boyfriend. So, all's fair in love and war, they say.' Dumesh laughed uncontrollably at this last statement.

The interview was terminated, and he was led back to his cell.

Dumesh was formally charged with 15 counts of murder, 15 counts of kidnap and false imprisonment, three counts of arson, two properties and a van, having a firearm in his possession, using it and the terror he had inflicted on two police officers, as well as the wasted police time by playing his so-called game. The charge of bribing Webster was dropped. Webster had resigned before he had been sacked and he had lost his wife and child. The CPS decided it was in nobody's interest that he be prosecuted. He had lost everything already.

Dumesh was in the holding cells awaiting transport to take him to a prison to await trial. The solicitor who had been with him was arguing that he should be psychologically tested and should be taken to Broadmoor instead. The CPS said there was nothing to confirm that he was mentally ill and that he would be treated accordingly. Whilst all this arguing was going on, Dumesh was scratching the number 16 into the floor of his cell. When he had gone for a toilet break and his solicitor had accompanied him, he had managed to steal his car keys from his jacket pocket. He etched the number 16 another 15 times on the wall. Then using his own shirt, he made a noose.

When an officer went to check on him and to tell him the transport was outside, he was found hanging. He had the number 16 etched all around him. The duty doctor was called, and he was pronounced dead at the scene.

Andrews looked at Thomas when they heard the news and said, 'Sixteen wasn't lucky for him, after all. He became his own sixteenth victim.'